Falling into real

Anne Colledge

Falling Into Fear

Anne Colledge

For Bob

Chapter 1 - All Change

Catherine's white-faced mother clutched a brown envelope. 'Recall. It says recall.'

'What's that?' Asked Catherine.

'I've got to go back to hospital for another test,' Mum said, 'You and Henry must go and stay with Granddad and Gran, while I get treatment.'

As soon as Mum said they must go away Catherine had a sinking feeling that strange things were going to happen when they were away; awful dangerous things. She meant to say, *I'll look after you, Mum*, but she shouted, 'I'm not going away. First Dad leaves and now this,' and banged out of the room.

When her friend Claire came she went straight up to Catherine's bedroom.

'Mum's sick again.' Catherine said.

'She'll be okay,' said Claire looking worried so it did not help.

'All summer wasted up North, and I won't see Richard or any of the others,' said Catherine.

'I'll write and tell you all the news,' Claire said.

'Thanks, that would be good.' Catherine said.

Mum took them up north in her car. The windscreen wipers went faster and faster getting rid of the heavy downpour. Catherine stared out over the moors and terraced houses, so different to London.

The car stopped in the back street. Gran was standing at the back door in the tiny back yard.

'Where's Dad?' asked Mum. Then she saw his feet sticking out from under the old blue Mini. He shot out wiping his hands on his trousers.

You could hardly get your arms round Gran who was plump. When you hugged Granddad you could feel his ribs through his warm shirt.

'Come in,' said Gran. 'The kettle's on for a cup of tea.' The table was laid with and ham and pease pudding, a thick yellow stuff you spread on ham. Catherine shuddered but ate it.

When Mum's car disappeared round the street corner, taking Mum back to London Catherine felt worried. Would Mum be all right on her own in London? She needed someone to look after her when she was ill.

There was a knock on the back door.

'Come in, the kettle's on,' called Gran. So many people visited that Gran said it was like Carrie's Café, but she enjoyed company.

'They come for your baking,' said Granddad as Gran cut into the homemade chocolate cake.

'I've brought James to see you,' said the slim fair-haired woman as she came into the kitchen.

James stuck his black curly hair round the door.

'Is it OK to bring my bike in?'

'Yes, of course, we don't want that new racing bike stolen.'

'It's as light as a feather.' James ran his hand lovingly over the handlebars.

'Sport crazy,' said Mrs Knowles.

Catherine noticed their hearing aids at once, because she wore two herself. As Mrs Knowles drank her tea she said, 'Everyone's deaf in my family except the dog. She can hear OK.' She nodded to Cindy, a black and white sheep dog, which was noisily lapping up a bowl of water Granddad had put down for her.

When they left, Gran said, 'Mrs Knowles signs for her husband who is profoundly deaf. She's the Rolls Royce of signing.'

'Rolls Royce? What's that?' Asked Henry.

'It's the best car ever made. It runs smoothly and that's how Mrs. Knowles signs,' said Granddad. 'James is a good signer too.'

Catherine nodded. She could hear a lot with her hearing aids and did not need to sign. Still she would like to learn. Perhaps James and Mrs Knowles would help her. They were the experts. That meant she could see James again.

'Penny for your thoughts,' said Granddad.

'Don't start with your teasing,' said Gran.

'Bet you were thinking about James,' said Granddad.

Catherine jumped. She had been wondering which pop star James reminded her of.

'All I'm saying is that he is a good-looking lad. Better than those London boys, I bet.'

'You would fight with a feather,' said Gran.

Catherine got out her phone. Dear Claire, Met James today, she began her text message.

Chapter 2 - The Bomb

When Catherine went up to her bedroom there was nothing in it except a large wardrobe. There were no posters or books about like her bedroom at home. The sheets were cold cotton and she shivered. Henry had put up a notice, 'No girls only boys allowed here,' on his door so she had put 'no boys only girls' on hers but her heart wasn't in it. Who wanted to come anyway? She didn't know anyone.

That night she fell into the past for the first time. As soon as she got into bed she fell down and down and down as if she was falling into a deep dark well.

♦♦♦

When she opened her eyes she was wearing thick warm pyjamas. She swung her legs to the floor, which struck cold because there was no carpet only a small rug. The room was bitterly cold so she pulled on a thick dressing gown hanging behind the door and slippers from under the bed.

She crept along the landing to the top of the stairs listening. There were no sounds. She crept carefully down the steep stairs pulling the scratchy wool dressing gown tightly around her and put her ear to the door at the bottom trying to hear what Mum and Dad were saying. Henry came and knelt beside her. He listened.

'What are they saying?' She asked.

'Evacuated,' Henry said slowly. 'What's that?'

'You get sent away,' said Catherine.

'We're being sent away from the bombs, Dad said, but Mum doesn't agree. They were shouting at each other.'

Catherine went cold. She hated Mum and Dad arguing and quarrelling.

The next week all the children in their school went by bus to Newcastle Railway station. They had luggage labels tied to their coats with their names on.

'They are treated like parcels, not children,' said Mum. 'We don't even know where they're going.'

'Only the government knows. It's a secret so the Germans won't find them. There is a war on,' said Dad slipping Catherine and Henry six pence each. It was a small silver coin as big as a thumbnail. He winked, letting them know they were not to tell Mum.

Catherine held her brown cardboard suitcase in one hand and clutched Henry with the other. In her suitcase were three pairs of cotton knickers, socks, two blouses and a cardigan. She did not have many clothes, just three of most things. Mum said 'one on, one off and one in the wash.'

It was hard to get clothes as they were rationed and you had to give coupons as well as money. Mum had used the wool from an old cardigan to knit her a new one. They had to pull the wool out and wash it and use it again.

They had their gas masks in square cardboard boxes slung on their backs. Catherine hated hers. It smelt of rubber when you put it on and made it hard to breathe, but they had to take them everywhere with them in case there was a gas attack.

'No parents on the platform,' shouted a large woman in green uniform.

Dad pushed both Catherine and Henry forward. 'Go on, both of

5

you, I wish I was coming, it'll be an adventure.' Mum had her cotton handkerchief out as if she was going to cry.

The train pulled out of the station in a cloud of steam and soon the small houses and factories gave way to green fields.

'Can we eat our biscuits now?' Asked Henry. They all had a paper bag with sandwiches in and a small bottle of pop. The food was soon gone.

At last the black steam train pulled into the station and juddered to a halt. Catherine jumped up pulling at the leather strap, which held the window shut, pulled it down and leant out to open the carriage door. The station platform was packed with children.

'Line up,' Miss Kerr, their headmistress, a large lady in a navy coat, shouted.

They followed her into a waiting room. Catherine stared at a red poster on the wall with a crown with an orb on it at the top. In gold capital letters, it said 'KEEP CALM AND CARRY ON.'

'Right. We're going to find people to take you in. Come on now, we must hurry. I've got to get someone to take you all before it gets dark and that won't be long.'

Outside the station Catherine looked for a car or bus to take them but there were none. They marched up the long road to the village. One by one all the children were found somewhere to stay. Catherine clutched Henry's hand tightly. It was getting dark.

Miss Kerr knocked on the last door in the street. A thin woman wearing an apron opened it.

'Excuse me, but can you take these two evacuees?'

'Course I can,' said Mrs. Musgrave throwing the door open wide. 'They're just in time for tea.' There was a big coal fire burning in the grate.

There were sandwiches and home-made scones with blackberry jam for tea. 'Home-made jam,' said Mrs. Musgrave. Catherine started to feel better.

A boy came in. He wore short trousers and a Fair Isle pullover. He stopped, glaring at Catherine and Henry.

'This is John, my son,'

'I hope there's something left for my tea'

'There's plenty for everyone. Go and wash your hands.' When he was in the kitchen she said, 'Take no notice of him. He's not used to sharing, being an only child.'

John ate his tea without speaking, then said, 'Will they still be here in the morning?'

'Course they will and we have to make them feel at home.'

'Huh,' John said and stamped off to bed.

Next day Mrs. Musgrave asked John to take Catherine and Henry to the beach. He did not speak all the way there, but stumped ahead showing them the way.

The waves crashed down at their feet as they picked up the thin razor shells. Catherine showed Henry how to throw flat stones so that they skipped along the water. Mrs. Musgrave had given them sticky sweets called gob-stoppers in a brown paper bag. They filled your mouth and they had a competition to see how long they could make them last. Catherine won because Henry crunched his with his teeth. John kept his to eat when theirs were all gone.

'What's that?' Asked Henry pointing to something blue bobbing in the water. The waves brought it in to their feet.

'It might be something to do with the war,' said Catherine. Henry nodded.

'What should we do?' He said.

Catherine rolled the object over with her foot. 'We'll take it to the police station,' she said. Carefully she picked it up. It wasn't heavy but wet and sandy. John said he would help her carry it, which did help.

They walked back up the beach and into the town where they saw the sign pointing to the police station. They walked in and went to the Enquiry window. A policeman said, 'What do you want?' Then he saw what Catherine and John were carrying. 'Serge, Serge,' he shouted.

The sergeant came out of a back room. 'What's up?' He said. Then he saw what Catherine was carrying. He went white and then red in the face. He snatched a fire extinguisher from the wall and pointed it at Catherine and John. 'A bomb. That's a bomb.'

Catherine and John put it down on the floor very carefully. The policeman picked it up and ran out of the back into the yard.

'Not there,' shouted the sergeant, 'it's too near the railway line and the London express is due any minute.

The policeman dashed back out to reappear with the bomb and then took it out to the front.

'Too near the main road and the bus will pass soon,' shouted the sergeant.

'Where can I put it, Sarge?' The sergeant looked puzzled himself.

When he came back in red in the face and sweating he asked, 'Where did you find it?' Catherine explained about walking along the beach. 'You should never touch things like that,' he said.

The door banged back and another fat policeman came in pushing his bike.

'You know when to keep out of things. There's been hell going on here,' said the sergeant.

'What's up?'

'A bomb, that's what's up. These kids brought in a bomb.'

'The one that's in the front?'

'Yes, how many bombs do you think we have here?'

'Don't worry about that. That'll not harm anyone. It's a target bomb used by the RAF. That'll not blow us up. It's just a dummy.'

'So. I don't have to phone the Bomb Disposal boys?'

'They'll not thank you for wasting their time.'

'I'll just put the kettle on and these kids deserve some biscuits. Come over by the fire and sit down,' he said to Catherine, Henry and John.

Yellow sparks flew out of the fire. 'Get the fireguard round that fire. We don't want any more excitement. We've had enough for one day,' said the sergeant.

Catherine felt she was going to enjoy herself, and they were getting on better with John now, which would help. She watched the yellow flames lick up the black coal and thought she could see pictures of galloping horsemen in the flames. Then she was falling again.

♦ ♦ ♦

She was back in the unfamiliar bedroom and it was morning. What had happened? Was it a dream? It all seemed so real and scary. She couldn't say anything to Henry, as he was younger than her. She did not want to worry Granddad or Gran. They might think she was barking mad! Maybe it was because she was worried about Dad not living with them any more and anxious about staying with Gran and Granddad in the

North East. She remembered the poster in the railway station. KEEP CALM AND CARRY ON it said. That was what she would have to do and just wait and see what would happen. She hoped it would not be too scary and she could cope with it all. If only she had a good friend to talk to. She had plenty in London but it was no good thinking about that now. It wouldn't help.

There was a terrible pounding in her head. She went downstairs to the kitchen where Granddad was frying bacon.

'It's them next door,' said Granddad . 'The Church.'

'Oh, the bell ringers.'

Granddad gave her a bacon sandwich. It smelt great. He bit into his causing brown sauce to drip out of the sides. 'A bacon sandwich will put most things right,' he said.

Chapter 3 - Back to World War 2

'One more cloth to brighten the glass,' said Gran.

Catherine groaned to herself. The more she rubbed the windows the more smears there were. At last it was done.

'Jobs, jobs, jobs,' said Granddad going out of the back door.

'It's all right for him,' said Gran. 'We'll make the Yorkshire pudding. I'll crack the eggs onto the flour and milk in the bowl. You beat them. James often drops in on Sunday for my puddings.' Catherine nearly dropped the bowl.

'That's nice,' she said.

'Look in the oven at the first batch of puddings.'

Catherine opened the oven and felt a blast of hot air on her face. The batter had risen to golden circles. 'Wow, they're great,' she said.

'It's the beating.'

Catherine beat and beat until her arms ached. There was a lovely smell of roast beef from the oven.

James came in. 'Just in time,' said Gran as Catherine put the

Yorkshire puddings on the table.

After dinner James taught Catherine some signs. 'Take care with this one,' he said. 'It's *lies*. You don't want to upset anyone by using the wrong sign.'

'I made the Yorkshire puddings,' Catherine said and he signed *lies*.

'What's all the laughter about?' Granddad asked as he walked in. 'The Air Show starts at two o clock. Why don't we go?'

They crushed into the mini and drove to the airfield. The engines screamed as one plane chased the other high into the sky at the Air Show. Catherine was glad her digital aid stopped the noise for her.

'It's a dog fight, like they used to fight in the War, against the Germans,' shouted Granddad over the noise.

They squinted upwards trying to keep the planes in sight. The first one broke away and swooped down, falling away, chased by the other.

'Great,' said James.

'It'll be more exciting up there,' said Henry. 'It looks like they're going to crash any minute.'

'No they're not,' said Catherine.

'You don't know everything,' said Henry, 'Even if you think you do, know all.'

'I like the Spitfires best,' said Catherine.

'Stop showing off about knowing about Spitfires, just because you've been reading that book about them,' said Henry pulling a face at her. She shook her head at him not answering which made him angrier.

'Catherine's always reading,' said Gran. 'You should read more, Henry, instead of playing football from morning 'til night.' Henry groaned.

They went to look at a Spitfire. It was small with wide wings and red, white and blue rings on the body. At the front was a propeller.

'There were no jet engines then,' said Granddad, running his hand down the plane's side. 'Beautiful plane this. The pilots loved the Spitfires in the War.'

'What a small cockpit,' said Catherine.

'Fancy going up and fighting in that,' said James.

'I'd like to! It'd be exciting!' said Catherine.

Gran shook her head, 'I don't think so, too dangerous,' she said.

Catherine imagined herself pulling on goggles and a leather helmet and climbing into the cockpit, starting the engine, crouching over the controls, and peering out of the cloudy Perspex window. Then feeling the plane rumbling along the runway and taking off on patrol searching the skies for enemy planes. Another plane came alongside. A German plane was firing at her. She put her plane into a steep dive, at the last minute yanking the joystick and just managed to pull out of the spin. Everything went black and she felt herself falling further and further down. Oh no, she thought, I am falling through time again, back into the past.

♦ ♦ ♦

When she opened her eyes she smelt an acrid smell of burning. Her eyes stung with smoke.

'What's that smell?' She asked.

'They're burning old oil in the drums by the river again. The smoke screen stops the German's bombing the ship yards because they can't see them from their planes through the black smoke,' said Mum. 'Come in for your tea now.' Catherine realized that she was back in the dangerous time of World War Two.

She looked round in amazement. She was down by the river Tyne in Newcastle. Her mother had just gone in to a small terraced house so she followed her in. The house was dark inside but there was a bright coal fire burning in the grate.

'You'll have to go and feed Jock,' Mum said. 'Remember not to show a light or they'll be down on us like a ton of bricks.'

Catherine went carefully down the front path. Luckily there was a moon so she could see a bit. She went over the road taking the heavy iron key out of her pocket. She kept glancing up at the sky looking for enemy bombers. Her mouth felt dry she was that nervous. Jock launched himself at her legs nearly knocking her over. She patted the dog's rough hair.

'Are you nervous too?' She asked. She put the bits of left over dinner in his metal plate, which clanged on the stone floor.

She turned. A black shadow was looming at the back door. A German soldier! But it was only Mum.

'Didn't you hear the air raid warning? We've got to go down the shelter,' Mum said. 'I was just going to make some more chips as well.

The lard was just right for frying.'

Catherine followed her through the yard, stumbling in the dark to a corrugated iron shelter, sunk into the ground. Mum pulled at a piece of cotton that was hanging over the entrance and they crept inside. Henry was sitting on the bunk bed. It smelt damp and musty. They sat on the small iron bed listening to the bombs dropping and the ack-ack guns firing back.

'Good job I can't hear so well,' said Catherine. 'All this noise is frightening.'

They smiled bleakly at her.

'May as well get the cards out and have a game to pass the time,' said Mum.

They were dealing the cards when everything went quiet.

'Oh, no,' said Mum. 'I hope the next bomb hasn't got our name on it.' They sat frozen, listening to the terrible whine, whistling and howling noises as the bomb came down. Catherine could feel Henry shaking with fear beside her. She wanted to say something to cheer him up. She tried to open her mouth but could not manage to speak. Then there was a terrible crash and the earth floor shook under their feet.

A siren wailed. 'That's the All Clear. Come on, let's get out,' said Mum. They scrambled out into the night and saw that yellow flares lit up the sky. There was smoke and flames everywhere. A gas main had been hit and the flames seemed to reach the sky. Bells from ambulances and fire engines rang out loudly. They ran to the front of their house and found that the house opposite had been hit. The crater left looked like the gap when a tooth has been pulled out. The whole of the front of the house had gone. You could see right into the bedrooms and the kitchen. Catherine could not believe they had played in one of the bedrooms only yesterday.

Then Catherine was running as fast as she could for the back of number seven. There were bricks and rubble where the road had been. She stumbled again and again, falling and scraping her hands. The key was cold under her fingers in her pocket. Miraculously the kitchen was still standing. She rammed the key in the lock. It was jammed. Then she looked at the window. All the glass was out and lay shattered on the floor. It did not take her a minute to climb carefully through, onto the sink and over the draining board.

'Jock,' she shouted. 'Jock, where are you? Here boy, here.'

She looked up and saw flowers hanging from the lampshade in the ceiling. They were the daffodils they had picked yesterday from the garden. The blast must have blown them up there.

There was no sound except the creaking of wood and a terrible burning smell. She tasted ash in her mouth. Her heart sank. He must have been killed. He always rushed to the door. She was just turning away when she noticed something white moving in the corner. It was Jock waving his black and white tail. She turned on her small torch and saw he was trapped under a large piece of wood. She pulled but could not move it. There was another piece of wood near and she pushed that under and pushed with all her might. She was frightened to pull too much in case the lot came on top of them. At last he was free and with one wriggle got out and jumped on top of her licking her face as if to say thank you. Then they were both running down the path.

The neighbours were out shouting to each other and peering down the seven-meter crater in the middle of the street.

'Where've you been?' Said Mum.

Just round the corner,' said Catherine. She dare not tell Mum what had happened because she would go mad.

'The bomb didn't explode,' said Mum.

'No we wouldn't be here if it had,' said a policeman. 'Stand back everyone. Don't get too close.'

Catherine saw something on the ground; it was a piece of shrapnel. She picked it up. It was still warm. That would be good for her collection and she could perhaps swap it for a shell case at school.

As she looked into the crater Catherine felt dizzy again.

♦ ♦ ♦

She heard a screaming noise and looked up. Then she was standing back at the Air Show. The noise was only the Spitfire going over again. She was glad to be back. The War was exciting but dangerous, but what did it all mean?

In the London Museum she had seen a notice that said The Key to the Future is in the Past. Perhaps that was it. She was sick of puzzles and riddles.

She tried her trick to stop herself worrying. Worry, worry, worry.

Stop worrying, she thought, but it did not work. It all started up again. How was Mum? Was she getting better or worse? Her head felt like one of those snow scenes that you shake up and the snow whirls round and round.

James was watching her. 'Are you all right?' He asked.

She nodded uncertainly. He put his arm round her and gave her a hug.

'Let's get some ice cream,' said Granddad.

'Did you have ice cream in the War?' Asked Catherine.

'No, only a quarter of sweets each because of the rationing, and no bananas or chocolate. What made you think of that?'

'I just wondered,' said Catherine, not wanting to give too much away.

When they got home she took Mrs. Cat on her knee and stroked her as she had stroked Jock back in the past. She felt better as she had then. Animals seem to know when you are worried.

'Your Mum's on the phone, come and speak to her,' called Gran.

'Hi, how are you?' she asked Mum. Catherine started to tell her about the trip to the air show.

'I can't talk long,' Mum said. Her voice sounded wobbly. Catherine's stomach tightened and she felt sick again. Gran called, 'Everything all right?' 'Yes,' Catherine called back, not wanting to worry everyone. She picked up her phone and sent a text message to Claire. Mum's not too good again. Can you go and see her?

It was not long before the message came back. 'OK.' Then another text came an hour later. 'She's OK. Had more treatment that's all.' Catherine felt better. She would rather know what was happening than be kept in the dark expecting the worst all the time.

Chapter 4 - The Dare

Something awful was going to happen that day. Catherine knew it as soon as she opened her eyes and looked round the bedroom. Mum was having her operation today. She and Henry were going canoeing because Granddad said that would take their minds off it.

'No point hanging around worrying,' he said.

The week before Henry said, 'I dare you to go over the weir.'

Catherine never refused a dare but her hand shook as she signed for the canoe trip with the two-meter drop over the weir.

It was cold but sunny when they arrived at the Canoe club ready for the trip. 'White water! I like the sound of that,' said Henry.

Catherine looked at the first drop the boats would go down. I like nice blue water, she thought 'I'll go in a bit lower down,' she said, dragging her kayak after her, feeling stupid.

James slithered down the bank. 'I'm helping on this session today. Let me help you with that.' He picked the kayak up, easily putting it on his shoulder, then he flicked up her paddle with his foot to catch it in his hand.

'Wow, how do you do that?'

'Just practice. It's easy. I'll show you when we get time later.'

Henry easily went over the white water, where the currents were fast, and did a racing turn to land in front of her. Then set off quickly again.

Catherine groaned, 'show off!'

'Take no notice. We'll practice you carrying the canoe on your shoulder and tossing the paddle up. That'll show him.'

James always seemed to be at her side as they paddled companionably down the river. She smiled up at him. He pointed to a seal that was swimming just behind them.

'I've never seen one so close,' Catherine said.

'I've got to go now. I'm on the river trip up to Scotland. See you later,' and James was gone paddling quickly up the river in his play boat.

Catherine paddled as hard as she could but she still seemed to end up last. Every time she caught up with the others they were off again. There was a blister starting on her thumb.

'There's a drop. Wait at the bank and go over one at a time when I call you,' shouted Sarah, the instructor. 'Catherine, come on.' As Catherine lined up her heart began to pound loudly.

'Paddle up, paddle up,' they shouted as she got near the edge. Her boat stuck on a rock. Sarah shouted, 'Paddle left.' Catherine tried but went backwards but at least she was moving. She laughed. This was fun. She flew past Henry's astonished face. Not to be outdone, he raced after her. A current caught him by surprise and he capsized.

Sarah went to rescue him. She heaved his boat over hers and the water gushed out.

'Get between the boats and put your feet in first,' she instructed.

Henry tried, but at the last minute slipped back onto the water. Sarah grabbed his lifejacket and hauled him in like a landed fish. He smiled sheepishly at Catherine.

Turning the corner of the river they heard the roar of the weir. 'Let's go over together,' Henry shouted. Catherine nodded. The front of the boats tipped steeply as they got to the edge but they leant backwards. It's only like going over the slide in the baths Catherine thought. The kayak bottoms scraped on the concrete then they were on the smaller drop. There was a quick rush through the white water that splashed up into their boats and faces then they were down and into the calm water.

She saw a blue flash out of the corner of her eye. It was a kingfisher. She had always wanted to see one. It flew up the river low on the water. At the end of its territory it turned and flew back down the path on the other side of the river so that she saw its orange front. That must mean good luck.

'Keep to the left as you go down the next weir,' shouted Sarah.

Catherine got down successfully but at the bottom she was so glad to have got down that she stopped paddling. The current dragged her in to the stopper at the foot of the weir. The water curled round and round, like a whirlpool holding her in the current so that she could not get out. She saw the others mouths wide open shouting advice but because of the noise of the water dropping down and her hearing loss she could not make out what they were saying.

Her kayak was leaning over to the left at a dangerous angle and the strong current at the bottom was dragging her into the middle of the river. She put her paddle out to the left to do a support stroke and it worked. She stayed upright. She had never done one successfully before but now she did. She got nearly to the other side of the river when the water started to pour down onto the other side of her boat. She pulled her spray deck, which kept water out of the boat, stood up and jumped into the water near to the instructor who was waiting to tow her in. After the first shock of the water she was warm in her wet suit.

On the flat rock with the others they saw her kayak dragged bobbing along in the stopper.

Sarah tied a rope round Henry and he waded in to get Catherine's boat.

Then they all got back into their boats to finish the trip.

Back at Shorebase Sarah said, 'who wants to do a capsize with spray deck on?'

'I will,' shouted Henry and threw himself in to pop up straight away.

'Want a go, Catherine?' Asked Sarah.

Catherine nodded. She was not keen but would have a try. When she went over the cold water was a shock but then she opened her eyes, pulled the spray deck off and she was out. *I did it*! she thought, pleased.

'You did great,' said Henry. Catherine smiled, what would the next dare be, she wondered? Anyway there was no time to worry about anything when you were canoeing.

Granddad was waiting for them at the clubhouse. He was smiling, 'Everything went well with your Mum's operation. She's fine,' he said. 'We're going for fish and chips to celebrate, then we'll come back and pick James up. He's on a difficult river trip. He's a four star canoeist now. You can't get much better than that.'

Catherine whistled in surprise, she was only a one star.

'He wants to go to college and work in a Sports Centre. I bet he falls asleep in the car going home. He gives 100% to his sports. Come on lets get the best fish and chips in the world.'

Chapter 5 - FIRE! FIRE!

'We'll go to Beamish tomorrow, Granddad said, 'Beamish Open Air Museum. Everything's like it was 100 years ago. You can ride on a tram or go down a coal mine.'

He took his miner's lamp down out of the china cabinet, rubbing it. 'This lamp went out to warn us if there was gas down the pit. The gas was a killer. Before the lamps they had canaries. If the canary was still singing we knew we were alright.'

'I wouldn't go down the pit,' said Henry.

'I'd go down now if the doctor would let me,' said Granddad. 'It's working with friends. That's the best.'

'Brush your hair, Catherine. It is short,' said Gran. 'Do you remember when you were little you used to say you were a boy so you could join in the games?'

Catherine nodded, laughing.

'You scored all the goals at football,' said Granddad. 'Better than the boys you were. Still are, I expect. It's not far to Beamish. There's no traffic jams like there are in London. Big cities are no good. I don't know why you went there.'

'They had to go for their Mum's work,' said Gran, shaking her head at him.

They were to Beamish in the blue Mini. Granddad revved the car up outside.

'Come on,' he shouted, impatient to be off as usual. It creaked and groaned with Gran's weight as she got in.

'Mind the springs,' Granddad said but Gran just laughed. Granddad pushed the car into gear and was off before they were settled. Gran gave Catherine a carrier bag full of food for the picnic.

'We're not going for a month,' said Granddad. 'Still this car carries anything. It's a real work horse.'

At the museum they ran to the cart, drawn by two horses, and climbed up into it. It rattled over the cobblestones shaking their bones. Catherine hung on to the side as she was thrown about so that her teeth chattered together.

'Great,' she shouted.

'Give me a car any day,' said Gran.

Catherine saw the old-fashioned Fair Ground with Swing Boats and golden Hobby Horses going up and down and round and round.

'Let's go to the Fair,' she said.

'No, the farm,' said Henry rubbing at the freckles which spread over his nose and pushing his cap back on his head.

'Calm down you two. We've got all day to do whatever we want,' said Granddad.

The cart stopped outside the coal miner's cottages.

Let's go in here,' said Gran.

They climbed out and walked up the garden path. On either side were neat rows of vegetables and hens scratched. They went round to the back door. The smell of bread baking was delicious in the hot kitchen with the banked up coal fire. Catherine sat on the hard wooden bench. She felt sleepy and shut her eyes.

◆◆◆

When she opened her eyes Gran was dressed in a long skirt.

'There you are,' said Gran. 'I need your help.' She pointed to the mangle, a heavy machine with big wooden rollers that squeezed water out of the washing. Gran was banging a copper object up and down on the clothes in a big tub to get the dirt out of them and rubbing the clothes with a green bar of strong smelling soap.

Catherine put a white cotton pillowcase in the wooden mangle, and then jumped on the handle to bring it down. The clothes were squeezed flat and all the water spilled out. Catherine felt the water splash on to her legs, which were covered in thick black stockings. Her long skirt got in her way.

'Time for school,' said Gran, as she went to peg the clothes on the line.

Catherine looked for her coat but there was only a shawl so she wrapped that round her shoulders, put on the cotton mob cap and smoothed down her apron which was a bit wet from the washing, but she couldn't help that.

She walked across the field to the school. It was a long squat one-storey building with two separate entrances with Boys and Girls over each. Catherine went in the Girls' entrance.

The big schoolroom had high windows and was filled with desks. She walked round the wooden desks placed in rows, carefully filling the white pot inkwells with ink from the big bottle. There were benches for the children to sit on at each wooden desk. The desks had lids and inside were slates for each child, with chalk and rags to clean them. At the front was a large black board for the teacher.

Catherine decided to try writing with the ink. The pen was a nib on a thin piece of wood. She dipped it into the inkwell. When she pressed the nib onto the paper the nib crossed and splattered in inkblots. She tried again, not pressing so hard this time and it was a bit better. Her fingers, where she had held the pen, were covered in ink and it didn't come off however much she rubbed at it.

The caretaker, Mr. Johnson, was on his knees laying sticks and paper in the big open grate, ready to light the fire, which was supposed to heat the large classroom.

'I'm usually finished by half past six, but my youngest, Maggie was sick for half the night. Well, you don't expect much sleep with nine children. There's Mr. Elliot coming. I'll slip out the back. He'll go mad if he catches me so late.' He emptied a bucket of coal on the fire that billowed out smoke.

Mr. Elliot, the headmaster, came in and stood beside his tall desk in his dark suit and shirt and tie.

'Ring the bell,' said Mr. Elliot glancing at his fob watch that he took from his waistcoat pocket.

Catherine ran first to the girls' yard and rang the heavy brass bell and then to the boys' liking the loud noise it made. The children stopped playing with their hoops or whip and tops and stood still, then quickly ran into lines and walked in without speaking.

When they were all sitting down after prayers Mr. Elliot said to Catherine, 'I'm going out. You're in charge.'

Catherine stood in front of the class wondering what to do, then she started to chant, 'One two is two, two twos are four,' and all the children joined in with singsong voices.

At half past nine the timetable said Silent Reading. Catherine helped the little ones, reading a story about a Little Match Girl, who sold matches because she was poor. Catherine wished for a more cheerful story. Billy came running up pulling at Catherine's apron.

'What is it, Billy? Sit down. You're not allowed out of your seat.'

Billy went on tiptoes whispering in Catherine's ear. She hated that. She could never hear anything. She pushed him back, so that she could lip-read.

'What is it Billy?'

'There's a fire.' Billy pointed to the flames that were already licking up the wooden wall near the fire. Catherine saw the fireguard was not round the fire. Mr. Johnson must have forgotten to put it back because of his hurry. A spark had fallen on to the dry wooden floor. Flames were licking up the walls.

Catherine stood in front of the fire. She felt frightened. What if the children panicked and they could not get out? She could see the flames getting a hold and spreading.

'I want you to walk quietly into the school yard.' Her voice was a bit quivery but the children did not seem to notice but got up quietly and filed out quickly.

Catherine checked the windows were all closed and shut the door after her to contain the fire. The children were standing white faced in the yard.

'Billy, run over to the Pit and tell them the school is on fire.

The rest of you line up.'

Catherine went back into the cloakroom for the red buckets. She filled one with water. Stan, stand here and fill the buckets then pass them along the line.'

Heat and smoke hit her in the face as she opened the classroom door but she threw the water on the fire reaching for another bucket. They heard the clang of the fire engine as the steaming horses galloped across the field.

The children cheered when the bright red fire engine trundled up.

Some firemen rushed in with the hose whilst others pumped away at the fire engine to raise the water pressure. The arcs of water splashed helplessly at first as the flames flew upwards. The men dragged at the long hoses to get nearer. At last the leaping orange and yellow flames gave way to a sullen smouldering. The children cheered again.

Mr. Elliot came rushing up, his hat knocked sideways in his rush, 'What's happened?' They all started to tell him at once.

'You'll have to be sent home until this is cleared up.' The children cheered loudly. Then Catherine felt dizzy. One of the firemen picked her up and carried her away from the smoke.

◆ ◆ ◆

When she opened her eyes she was going into one of the cottages with Gran, Granddad and Henry dressed in ordinary clothes again.

'Have we been in this house before?' She whispered to Henry. He shook his head, puzzled.

There was a delicious smell of baking bread made by a woman dressed in a long skirt as Catherine and Gran had been before Catherine came back to the present.

Catherine nudged Henry, 'Have we been here long?' She asked. He gave her a look, 'No,' he said. Catherine sniffed her hand, sure she could smell smoke on it. She was happy in the little cottage with Gran. They could have a good time until Mum came to take them home. It was no use worrying anyway. That would not help, and she was having some strange adventures.

Chapter 6 - The Lost Ring

They were on their way to South Shields to visit Arbeia, the Roman fort with its huge gateway with two arched doors and twelve arched windows.

Catherine was worrying again. Is Mum's illness dangerous? Catherine thought. Was it life threatening?

She heard Gran talking on the phone to Mum that morning.

'You'll be all right.' Gran said. 'When do you get the test results?'

Tests, results, Catherine felt sick and walked away. 'They can do wonderful things now,' was something people said. Everything was going round in her head and she didn't know what to think.

As if he had guessed her thoughts Granddad turned off the road and pointed. There on a hill was a huge angel with wings like an enormous plane. 'The Angel of the North,' he said proudly. 'We'll take a photo. That'll cheer your Mum up.' Catherine stood beside the angel with her arms out and Henry pulled a face as usual.

The white spray crashed over the sea wall whipped up by the cold wind onto the shore as the Mini drove slowly along the road, which ran parallel to the shore.

'Beautiful coast line,' said Granddad. 'They call this the Secret Kingdom. For centuries it was two kingdoms and when the borders were fought over it left us with more castles than any other English county. If you add on the towers there are seven hundred. People still live in Bamburgh Castle and that is where Harry Potter's first film was shot.'

'Wow,' said Henry staring out of the window.'

Inside Henry said, 'Hold my anorak while I get my camera out.'

'I'm not your slave,' Catherine answered.

She looked down at her feet down at the thin white bones of the skeleton lying on the earth in its narrow coffin sunk into the floor of the museum. The bones were thinner than she expected. There was money and a bowl for the man to use in the next world. The bones of the fingers were not joined on to the hands any more. She looked into the eye sockets and felt the familiar dizziness, and then she was falling back into the past again.

♦♦♦

She sneezed.

'Bana salus, good health,' she heard.

She looked up to see Flavia, a beautiful Roman woman, dressed in a blue flowing robe reaching down to her feet. Her long black curly hair was tied back and she wore three necklaces. She looked at Catherine kindly.

'Thank you, mistress,' she replied.

Catherine was in a courtyard, open in the middle with a small rectangular pond. Brown pillars rose from the white walls and the roofs were sloped and covered in brown tiles. The walls were painted with pictures of trees, birds and flowers in brown, blue and green.

'Come,' said Flavia, 'I need to speak to you privately.'

Catherine followed her through the door into a room with a high ceiling and two oval windows. Plump cushions covered wooden seats.

'Sit beside me, Catherine.' Flavia gave her a spindle. 'Spin while we are talking in case someone comes in. It will look strange otherwise if you are doing nothing.'

Catherine picked up the spindle and began to tease out the soft grey greasy sheep's wool into threads and wind them on the bobbin.

'I am in trouble,' whispered Flavia.

Catherine hated it when people whispered because then she could not hear properly.

'Please speak up, mistress,' she said.

Flavia glanced carefully around making sure no one could hear and began to speak more clearly. 'I'm in trouble,' she said.

'I'm sorry to hear that,' said Catherine because already she liked Flavia and wanted to help her.

'I have lost something precious,' said Flavia. 'I will tell you my story, so you understand what the object means to me, and how important it is to my life at the Fort.'

'My father arranged my marriage when I was 13 years old,' began Flavia.

Catherine gulped. She could not imagine being married so young.

'Yes,' said Flavia, 'I was just about your age. At my home my father signed the contract. We had prayers and a special cake my mother made to be offered to the gods and goddesses.'

'What was your dress like?' asked Catherine.

'It was white and I had an orange shawl over my head, like the flames in the torches the people carried in procession. My husband and I joined hands and I said, 'Where you are master I will be mistress.' Then he put the gold ring made into the shape of two hands joined together onto my finger.'

'Nice,' said Catherine.

'Yes. Then there was a great feast, with wine and fruit and good food. It was a wonderful day. I was not married here but in my own beautiful country where it is warm and sunny. Not like here,' she shivered. 'With the cold north winds and the rain.'

Catherine nodded, 'Why are you worried?'

Flavia frowned and held out her hand, previously hidden in the folds of her robe. The finger where her gold wedding ring with two clasped hands should be was bare. Catherine nearly cried out in surprise but Flavia put a warning finger to her lips.

'Yes, my wedding ring, is lost,' said Flavia. 'My husband will be angry if he finds out. He is already in a bad mood because the soldiers are complaining about the cramped quarters they have to live in. I cannot tell anyone in the fort other than you. I do not trust them. Because my husband is Commander of the fort people are jealous of us and would like to make our lives more difficult for us. They are jealous of our large, beautiful house when they have so little.'

Catherine nodded. 'I understand.'

'If you find the ring I will make you a free woman. You will no longer be a slave. I am allowed to do that. Please, tell no one. I trust you.'

'I will help,' said Catherine not knowing how but Flavia looked so worried she would have to try.

'I am going to the Bath House,' said Flavia. 'So that no one will notice my missing ring.'

Catherine went into the large room shaking the cushions, searching under each one, but there was no ring. She went into the kitchen to grind herbs for the evening meal but could not concentrate. She had to find the ring before dinner, as it was impossible for Flavia to hide her hand over dinner. Catherine went from one end of the villa to the other searching every room but found nothing. She heard her master come in.

'Girl, come here at once,' he shouted. She nearly dropped the goblet she was holding.

'Coming, Master.'

'Where is your Mistress?'

'She has gone to the Bath House, Master.'

'She should be at home when I come.' The Commander's face darkened and he stamped into his office, slamming the door.

It was almost too late. Flavia would soon come home from the Bath House. Catherine had to go to the Latrine. She had not been all afternoon.

There was no moss left in the latrine so she went to pick dock leaves instead. She saw a glint of gold in the leaves. She stooped to pick the object up when she saw a dark spider beside it. Ugh. She hated spiders. She could stand mice but not spiders. It's just a little thing, she thought, but then she shuddered thinking of the eight hairy legs. She remembered Latvia's worried face. It was a pity that Henry was not there, he would help her. He usually caught the spider in a towel and put it outside, charging her a pound each time he did it. She would do it herself. She took some material from her long robe and picked up the spider and put it down further away where it would not bother her, and bent down brushing the spider away and grasped the ring.

She held it tightly creeping down the corridor past the master's room. Luckily the door was still shut. It flew open.

'What are you doing, girl?' Shouted the Commander.

'Just seeing to the dinner, Master,' she said slipping into the kitchen. The door banged. She began to panic. She should be serving the dinner soon and her Master was already in a bad temper. What excuse could she give if dinner was not on time? She was not allowed out of the fort. After a minute, with a pounding heart she crept past the Master's door again.

This time she got safely out and ran as fast as she could to the Bath House. She slipped through the large door past the pillars into the first bath chamber. The walls were arched and high and there were many women sitting in or at the side of the bath. It was steamy and difficult to see. Catherine looked round for her Mistress. At last she saw her sitting alone looking miserable.

'Mistress, Mistress,' Catherine called and slipped the ring into her hand. Latvia's eyes lit up with joy as she saw the gold ring with the two clasped hands.

'I knew you would help me, Catherine,' she said, putting the ring back on her finger. 'I am so happy to get it back.' Then Catherine felt the dizziness again.

◆◆◆

When she opened her eyes she was back beside the skeleton feeling frightened again as she looked into the eye sockets.

Henry said, 'Go on hold my anorak a minute.'

Catherine said, 'What do you think I am your s....' but thought better of it. She knew the meaning of being a slave now.

'I'm going to the Latrine,' she said making for the toilet. They stared at her.

'What did you say?' asked Henry, but she was disappearing into the toilet. At least there was toilet paper in there, not moss on a stick, or dock leaves. Some things are better in our century.

Driving home along a winding road with trees on either side in the dusk Catherine looked up and saw a white owl swoop in front of the car. As it flapped past she saw the flecks on the wings and each flight feather stretched out and the round flat face.

'It's a Barn Owl,' she said. It's lucky to see one, because there are fewer barns for them to nest in on the farms now.' It was like a white ghost.

'I don't know about lucky to see one,' said Granddad. 'They used to say it was bad luck to see one. They brought bad news.'

'Get away with you,' said Gran. 'I never heard such nonsense.'

Catherine shivered. She hoped the bad news was not about Mum.

Chapter 7 - Fools' Gold

The windscreen wipers went faster getting rid of the heavy downpour. Catherine stared out over the moors and terraced houses, so different to London.

'Nearly there.' Said Granddad. 'Killhope Lead Mine is a great day out. At least the rain's stopped. Lots to do. Better hurry. The sky looks black as if it might thunder later.' Catherine nodded.

In the lead mine Catherine went to the waste stones beside the huge water wheel where, one hundred years ago, boys separated lead ore from rock. She lifted the heavy hammer above her head bringing it down, smashing the stone as splinters flew everywhere. Great. She lifted the hammer to smash it down again. She was enjoying this.

◆ ◆ ◆

As she raised the hammer someone grabbed her arm, roughly, stopping her. She looked round expecting to see Mum or Henry but there was a man in dark trousers with a scarf round his neck, wearing a cloth cap. He shook her, 'Get to work, lad. Catch up with Tom.' he shouted. Catherine looked down at her feet in amazement. Her trainers had changed to clogs, her jeans to baggy trousers and her tee shirt to a long sleeved grey flannel shirt. Lad, Catherine thought, does he mean me? Who's Tom? There was no time to worry about it.

A boy who looked about eleven shouted, 'Come on,' and disappeared through a grating in the wall, the mine entrance. Catherine saw her brother Henry slipping and sliding down the muddy path towards her holding bread and a water bottle. 'You forgot these,' he said, 'so Mum sent me with them.

'Tom jumped into the water. 'Come on, lad,' he said to Catherine. 'We must keep up, or we'll lose them.' Catherine followed him into cold water up to her ankles. He must think I'm a boy because of my short hair and trousers, she thought.

A stream disappeared into the mountainside. Inside it was dark and the floor sloped steeply. They walked fast to keep up with the men in front, stumbling over stones and boulders in the streambed.

'What's up with you today?' Asked Tom.

'I can't see,' said Catherine.

''Ere your candle's not lit,' said Tom. There was a flare and Tom lit a candle in her cloth cap. 'Hurry up now, or there'll be trouble.' Tom turned sharp right down another black tunnel. Catherine struggled after him not wanting to be left behind.

'How do you find your way?' she asked.

'I follow the noise from the pump,' Tom replied. Catherine strained to hear him because she did not have her hearing aids on. She felt the wet bricks on the wall for the vibration. Thump, thump, thump went the pump. That would help. She would have to depend on her memory and her hands to find the way. She ran her hand down a deep groove in the rock. The walls ran with water.

'Aye,' Tom said. 'The water's the most dangerous for us. Once I was up to my neck in black cold water. If it rains heavy, it floods down here.'

Catherine shuddered.

'It's all right,' Tom said cheerfully. 'I always get out. Always have. Come on.'

He began to run and Catherine stumbled over the rough stones after him. She wanted to turn and run back to the surface. She couldn't breathe but she didn't know the way back and she couldn't let Tom down. She took a deep breath, forcing herself to go further into the mine.

They came to the huge water wheel that was pumping water out of the mine. The noise was deafening in the small space. There was a white sturdily built pit pony patiently waiting with its head down for a wagon to be filled with stones. Tom picked one up and gave it to Catherine. She dropped it, just missing her foot. 'It's so heavy it could break your leg.' she said, 'It's as heavy as...'

'Lead,' laughed Tom. 'Let's get this wagon filled then Pip will take it up.'

She stroked the pit pony expecting the hair to be rough: it was soft but thick with dust.

'He's well looked after. Bill brushes him every night at the end of the shift. Pip's a favourite with everyone.'

A big worn leather yoke around Pip's neck pulled the wheeled tubs. He had an iron cage over his eyes.

'What's that for?' She asked.

'Keeps the stones off his eyes in a fall, and the one over his mouth stops him eating our sandwiches,' Tom laughed. 'He rolls in the mud on the surface and gets black.'

They worked for hours until Catherine's back ached from throwing stones into the wagons, which were then pulled to the surface by the ponies.

At twelve o clock a whistle went for the dinner break. The bread was the best Catherine had ever tasted. They swigged from the water bottles.

Tom glanced round. 'Want to see something?' he asked. Catherine nodded. Tom led her down a narrow passage off to the left. Suddenly they were at the entrance to a huge cave. Tom disappeared. Catherine thought he had slipped over the edge but then she saw a ladder. The worst part was going over the edge, but she wasn't going to be left behind. She hung on to the iron rungs and scrambled down.

They were in an enormous cavern where shining crystals glittered in the roof and walls from the light from their candles. Catherine shivered as the sweat dried on her shirt. Tom picked up a glittering stone

and gave it to her. 'Gold,' Catherine said. Tom shook his head, 'Fools' gold, but there is silver here and it's made some people rich.'

Catherine saw a huge wheel on the ground. 'What's that?'

'The old winding wheel,' said Tom. 'It was up in the roof. Good job we weren't here when it fell. Come on; let's get back to work before they miss us. We're not allowed in the caves. Too dangerous.'

They had just started to work again when Tom stopped and listened. 'It's quiet. The pump's stopped.'

The foreman came blundering up. 'Run up to the surface you two. Tell them the pumps stopped and the mine's flooding. Hurry or we'll never get the men out in time.'

Tom was off with Catherine after him. The stream was as thin as a needle down the first passage, but began to rush and bubble over their clogs as they went on. 'Must be raining heavy on the surface,' said Tom.

'It's a flash flood,' said Catherine.

'Could be a thunder storm.' Tom ran, slipping and slithering in the water. Catherine's foot slipped on a wobbly rock and she fell on her knees in the water. She felt a sharp pain in her ankle.

'You all right?' Called Tom.

'OK,' said Catherine.

They came to a ledge. Catherine kept her back to the wall. It was a six-foot drop. She must not look down. A stone dislodged under her foot and there was a fall of stones and loose rocks, which took a long time to get to the bottom.

Tom stopped and Catherine bumped into him. 'What's the matter?' She asked.

'Which way is up?' Tom answered. They stared at the three passages. 'Men have been lost down here,' muttered Tom. 'My Uncle Tom, who I'm named after, was.' She shivered putting her hand on the rock. Then she felt it, the deep cuts.

'This way,' she shouted.

'How do you know?'

'There are deep cuts down the rocks. I felt them on the way in.'

'Aye, the old miners made them, to guide them on their way, then went down in the dark to save candles,' said Tom.

Catherine went first, bent double, but they still cracked their heads on the roof despite their thick cloth caps. Catherine felt a drop roll down her forehead. Was it blood, sweat or water? There was no time to find out. She was sweating and panting. How long could she keep going? She had a stitch in her right side.

The water was getting deeper. 'Are you sure this is the right way?' Tom asked.

'Sure.' The stream was deep icy water up to their necks now. Then it became shallow again. She crept forward with the rock on her stomach but she did not feel so frightened. She felt she would be OK. Perhaps it was because her Granddad was a miner and it was in her blood to go underground.

She looked up and saw a pinhole of daylight. The surface! They ran out of the mine, back through the grating in the wall, to the foreman's hut and raised the alarm.

'Right, I'll send men down to get the pump working to drain the flood water. Good work, lad, the mine floods fast. The men would have died if you hadn't been so quick'

Catherine and Tom lay on the ground panting for breath. The storm was over and the sun came out. The fresh air smelt good.

Tom said, 'It's beautiful here.' He reached and picked a flower that grew all round them. 'It's a Mountain Pansy,' he said, 'purple with yellow at its heart. It'll grow only here.'

'Why?' Asked Catherine. 'It's the iron in the soil that also gives us work,' said Tom.

Catherine felt tired and shut her eyes.

♦♦♦

'Catherine,' said Henry. 'Gran's been looking for you. Where've you been?' Catherine was dressed in jeans and tee shirt again. 'Gran's in the cafe,' said Henry. Catherine followed him.

'Where've you been?' Asked Gran. Catherine slipped her hearing aids on, glad to have them back.

'What's the matter?' Asked Henry? 'You've gone white.'

'That old photograph.' She pointed to the wall. It was the wheel she had seen in the underground cavern, but it was hanging from the ceiling.

'Just an old photograph,' said Henry.

She put her hand in her right pocket and brought out a rock. It glittered.

'Gold,' said Henry.

'No,' she said, 'Fools' gold.'

'Come on,' Henry said, 'we're going down the mine. You get a hard hat and wellies.' Catherine shook her head. 'No, I'm not going down that mine again,' she muttered. She stared at another old photograph of a group of boys and girls. No wonder they mistook her for a boy. The girls had shoulder length hair with skirts down to their feet. Only the boys wore trousers.

Catherine hung back wanting time to think. What had happened? She didn't know. She closed her hand over the fools' gold. Had she been dreaming? What did it all mean?

Tom had been a good friend. She looked at her mobile phone. There was a new text message. She bet it was from Claire. She had lots to tell her. Mysterious things were happening in the North East. What would happen next, she wondered?

Chapter 8 - The White Mother Wolf

The blue mini rattled down the road over the moors.

'What's that?' Catherine asked pointing to the roundhouse made of stone at the bottom, with a thatched roof and surrounded by a stockade.

'It's a roundhouse like the Celts lived in, in Roman times,' said Granddad.

The car bumped over the road and Catherine felt herself falling again.

♦ ♦ ♦

She and Henry were walking up the path to the roundhouse and it felt good to be going back home. She could see the five-foot wall with the sharpened sticks, which kept out animals and intruders.

It was quiet and she realised she was not wearing her hearing aids.

She would have to lip-read which was tiring.

She pushed open the rough wattle door and saw the floor was beaten earth and there was a high roof. Gran squatted in the middle of the hut stirring a pot on the wood fire. Catherine and Henry sat on a plank of wood at the side of the fire.

'Tell us a story Gran,' said Catherine.

Grandmother rubbed her eyes. 'The smoke makes them sore,' she said. 'Which story would you like?' She settled on her haunches.

'A story about the wolves,' Henry said.

'I saw them two days ago up by the cave, by the big rocks and boulders.' She waved her arm towards the back of the round house. 'Outside their den the pups played and rolled in the sun, licking, pulling at each other and wagging their tails.

'A huge bear came. The White Mother Wolf charged immediately and drove him back. I could see puffs of dust at their feet as they raced down the slope. Suddenly the bear turned and chased the wolf. They stopped and faced each other again, staring for a few seconds. Then the wolf turned and walked calmly away. The bear stood on his hind legs sniffing the air, watched all the time by the White Mother. Then the bear charged again towards the den and the cubs. The wolf ran to meet him and they stared at each other again. The wolf turned and walked back to the den. The bear ambled down to the stream. The bear was three times as big as the wolf yet the wolf had won. Then her mate, the large Black Wolf, came with food for the cubs. They are mostly together those two wolves.'

Catherine stood up, 'We'll go for a walk now.'

Gran nodded, 'Yes. Take care. Above all do not go near the wolves. White Mother Wolf has cubs and she will do anything to defend them. Remember how she turned on the black bear. Keep away from their lair. When I was a child we used to play in that cave behind the rocks before the wolves came. It is warm and dry in the cave so is a good place to bring up the cubs safely. Remember to respect the wild animals and you'll come to no harm.'

They stopped outside the hut to listen. A loud howl echoed round the hills. It was the large Black Wolf. He stood on the hilltop, put back his head and howled. His neck stretched, his black nose was in the air, ears back, and his mouth open to show his fangs. His howl made them shiver. He was answered by another howl nearby. He turned and slipped away over the hill.

'He's gone for food for the cubs. They're always hungry,' said Catherine.

'Let's go to the wolves' den now,' said Henry.

Catherine nodded and they turned towards the big rocks. Catherine stopped so suddenly that Henry bumped into her. She pointed at the floor.

In the mud of the path they saw a huge paw print.

'What is it?' asked Henry.

'It's Black Wolf's foot print. He's the biggest of them,' said Catherine. She put her hand into the print: it was half the size of the foot.

They settled behind a gorse bush to watch the cubs, down wind so the wolves could not smell them.

The cubs liked to play by a broken tree stump below the cave. They named the cubs Snapper, Black Ear and Roller.

The cubs appeared at the mouth of the cave and rolled and fell down to the tree stump.

Snapper knocked Black Ear over with a swift blow from his paw. Black Ear rolled downhill, landing with the breath knocked out of him. He picked himself up, shook himself then licked the loose soil from his fur with a small pink tongue.

The other cub slipped down the bank, yelping, whimpering and wailing in fright as he knocked into loose rocks a and bushes. Snapper grabbed his ear and pulled and tugged at it with his sharp teeth clenched together. Roller wailed until he let go.

'They're learning to hunt for food when they play like that,' whispered Catherine.

Snapper bit Black Ear's tail until he squeaked. Black Ear hid behind a rock and jumped out on Snapper.

Henry laughed, 'that's what I do to you. Jump out and give you a fright.'

The three cubs rolled together until you could not tell which was which.

White Mother appeared at the cave mouth. She had a long thin face with amber eyes on each side of the long snout and nose. She was big, about two foot high and three foot long. Her ears were long and pointed. Catherine and Henry had watched her for a long time, before she had the cubs. She used to lie outside the cave in the sun curled up like a dog.

She whined but the pups took no notice of her. She trotted down to where they were playing whining for them to follow her. Black Ear rolled on his back and she licked his fur with her soft tongue.

She knocked Snapper with her sharp nose and swiped at Roller with her strong paw.

She regurgitated food from her own stomach for the cubs. She looked up noticing Catherine and Henry and went back into the cave followed by the cubs.

'It's as Gran says,' said Catherine. 'The wolves would rather walk away than cause trouble.'

When they disappeared into the cave Catherine and Henry walked on through the reeds and rushes, the yellow buttercups brushing their legs as they walked.

Suddenly Henry stopped, putting his hand up to warn Catherine. She couldn't hear anything but he pulled her down from the path to hide and soon after, six Roman soldiers marched past up to the Roman Fort.

The sky was blue turning to red as the sun sank. They saw two Roman soldiers silhouetted against the red sky. 'Red sky at night, shepherd's delight,' Gran said. It would be a fine day tomorrow.

The soldiers' metal helmets covered their heads and necks so that only their faces showed as they stood clutching their twelve-inch, sharp, pointed spears. They were watching for Scottish invaders coming to steal cattle. They did not bother about Catherine and Henry watching from behind the blackberry bush. Their father paid a percentage of his crops to feed the soldiers at the fort in return for protection from the Scots.

'It's the one with the black beard,' whispered Catherine. Henry nodded. The soldier's chain mail protected him and he had small brown eyes, which were always nervously looking over his shoulder. He kept touching his sword, his hand twitching, nervously, as if he was ready to use it immediately.

The gate of the fort opened and Claudia, wife of the Officer in Charge, came out holding hands with her little daughter, who was unsteady on her feet, as she had just learnt to walk. Claudia stopped to talk to her husband. Shiny yellow buttercups glittered in the long

grass outside the fort. The child toddled down to pick some. No one bothered that she had wandered off, as the Fort was safe. It was the last Fort in the Roman Empire and there was little trouble there, so the soldiers had never been on high alert and now they chatted amongst themselves not paying attention to what was happening.

Catherine noticed the white wolf trotting over the grass, coming towards them. At last she was so close that she heard the sharp intake of the wolf's breath and smelt on the wind the strong animal smell given off from her. She saw the sharp yellow teeth and long white hair of her pelt and the glittering eyes as White Mother slunk nearer through the grass.

Catherine knew that the Mother Wolf was on her way home to feed her cubs with the food already chewed for them, warm in her stomach ready to be regurgitated for them. They would be hungry watching every moment for her return.

The Romans feared wild animals and Catherine was frightened that the Roman soldiers would launch their deadly spears against White Mother Wolf. She was especially afraid of the nervous soldier who always seemed ready to launch his spear. She imagined them falling in a killing hail. She had seen deer hunted and killed by the deadly spears. She must not think of that now. Where would the cubs and Black Wolf be if he killed their mother?

The White Mother wolf stopped in her tracks, as if deciding what to do. She hesitated, her right front paw held in the air and looked at Catherine with her peaceful brown eyes, seeming to trust her.

Catherine whispered to Henry, 'Keep down. Stay here whatever happens.'

She ran down the slope to where the child played. The soldiers on the Fort raised their spears but still she ran and snatched the child, running back up the hill with her to her parents.

Claudia froze in terror to see the white wolf so near but the wolf turned and made off into the country, slipping away like a grey shadow almost hidden in the deep grass. Claudia clutched her daughter to her thanking Catherine in her strange language.

Her husband called a soldier and he came with a huge leg of venison, which they gave to Catherine. Henry had to help her to carry it home, because it was so heavy

Gran was standing at the door looking for them as they had been away so long. Her eyes sparkled at the sight of the venison and they put it in the hole in the ground in the hut to keep fresh. It was so big that it stuck out at both ends. It would make a good feast for all the family and Grandmother added the story to all her other wolf stories to tell on winters nights around the fire.

♦♦♦

'Eat your crusts up,' said Gran, 'they'll make your hair curl.'

They were sitting in the museum café eating sandwiches.

Catherine started to laugh.

'What's the joke?' asked Granddad.

'Mum told me that you always told her that and she ate the crusts and her hair is still straight.'

She ate her crusts up. The adventure had made her hungry.

Chapter 9 - Durham

The back door flew open and James came rushing in, grinning happily.

Catherine felt the whole kitchen had been lit up by bright sunlight.

'Do you want to come to Durham?' He asked Catherine.

She nodded emphatically.

'Is it okay if I go Gran?'

'Yes, you go and enjoy yourselves.'

They went on the train, which was fun.

'There it is,' said James. 'The most beautiful building in the world. Durham Cathedral.'

'It looks like the castle cakes Gran used to make me with ice cream cones for turrets for my birthday,' said Catherine.

'You lucky thing. My Gran never made me anything like that. She's too busy going to Bingo with her friends. I don't blame her,' said James.

The cathedral stood on a hill next to the castle with four square, strong towers. It had stone turrets and towers, high up looking down on the small houses crowded onto the narrow streets.

'Let's walk beside the river first,' James said.

They walked along the green riverbank in the dark shade of the trees. Catherine walked ahead and slithered down to the waterside. The water flooded past like thick brown coffee.

She did not know who was more surprised, her or the creature, which appeared beside her left foot staring up at her. They looked at each other both startled for a minute. The animal had a flat face. It turned its powerful body then slipped back down into the water with a swish of its long flat tail. In a way she was a bit disappointed that the animal's tail made it look a bit like a rat. It was an otter, she was sure of it although she had never seen one before. Dad had told her how he watched otters building dams in the river Dee in North Wales when he was a boy. Then how they went away because of the pollution. She had always wanted to see one. Her eyes filled with tears because it reminded her of all the good times she had had with her Dad before he went away.

She heard James slip down the bank to land beside her. 'What's wrong?'

'I just saw an otter.'

'That's a good thing. It shouldn't upset you.'

'It reminded me of my Dad. How he used to tell me things before he left us. My Dad used to talk to me about otters. He saw them when he was a boy in Wales. I miss my Dad now he doesn't live with us any more, but I can't say anything to Mum because it would only upset her,' she said.

'Of course you do. My Dad doesn't live with us now. You get used to it after a bit. You will get to see him when he comes on visits. I go to watch Sunderland play football with my Dad most Saturdays. We've got Season tickets. Mum doesn't mind. She just thinks we're crazy.'

'I think you're crazy as well. I'd like to see my Dad sometimes. I like football and so does he.

'Ask your Mum if you can go.'

'Yes, I will when Mum is a bit better. Am I going mad or what? All these dreams and going back into the past?'

'Course not. Don't be silly. I often dream when I'm worried about something. Sometimes it helps me to work things out and decide what to do.' He dragged her back up the bank. 'Come on, we've got to look at the cathedral.'

They walked up the steep cobbled street. Her body slumped. Then she felt James behind her and he pressed her right leg with his so that they marched together, one behind the other. People turned to look at them, smiled, then laughed. She felt better; she could not help it.

'Last time I was here,' said James, 'we went on a tour round the cathedral. The guide told us about the sanctuary knocker. In olden days people could go and seek sanctuary in the cathedral if people were chasing them. If you held the knocker they had to leave you alone and you could stay in the cathedral for a bit.'

The cathedral towered up to the sky. An ugly, evil looking, gargoyle glowered down at her. Catherine shivered as she put her hand on the cold metal doorknocker. It was in the shape of a face with a large straight nose with lines under the eyes and a large mouth. Black strands of hair stood up around its face and it was difficult to tell if it was human or an animal. The eyes were deep holes. As she stared into these she felt herself falling.

♦ ♦ ♦

She looked around to see there were fewer houses and lots of big oak trees. There was no sign of James or anyone else. She was alone. She heard a noise. It was faint like a horn being blown a long way away in the deep wood. She began to walk into the forest away from the cathedral to see if she could see what was happening in the forest. It was cool, dark and quiet in there. The large green fronds of ferns along the path sides brushed against her legs.

She stopped in a clearing and had a strange feeling that she was not alone. It was dark because the trees were dense but the sun shone through the leaves with a dappled light. She felt something watching her and made out two brown shining eyes looking at her. Not far away against a large oak tree was a small fawn standing with its mother. The fawn was brown with small spots and had thin delicate legs. It was not frightened but ripped at the succulent grass with her strong teeth and nibbled contentedly beside her mother.

Catherine felt suddenly hungry herself and sat down beside a blackberry bush and popped some berries in her mouth. They were juicy and she licked the juice from her fingers, which were stained by the black juice. She heard another blast from the horn, nearer now and the bay of hounds.

The fawn lifted her head and became tense suspecting danger. There was more noise of men crashing through the woods on horse-back, cracking whips and shouting.

Catherine looked at the fawn knowing she had to do something. She called out softly, 'Come with me, I know where we will be safe.'

The fawn looked at her with her clear brown eyes, then back at her mother as if deciding what to do.

The dogs broke into the clearing, barking and baying as they broke down the undergrowth. The leader of the pack stopped and bared his teeth letting out a low growl. Catherine felt cold at the sound.

The mother deer leapt into the air and ran back into the forest, trying to lead the dogs away from her fawn. Some followed but others still chased the fawn, and Catherine as they ran back down the path to the cathedral.

One huntsman dragged cruelly on his reins. His horse was sweating and foaming at the mouth.

'I want that deer on my table this evening for my dinner,' he shouted.

Catherine shuddered. As she put her hand on the knocker to open the cathedral door she saw the fawn leap over the wall into the cathedral grounds.

The huntsmen reined in their horses, disappointed, cracking their cruel whips at the hounds.

'Back,' they shouted, 'we cannot go in there. Curses on you girl for interfering with our sport.'

'Sport? Is that what you call it,' shouted Catherine.

They crashed back into the forest the way they had come.

The sun came out and it was suddenly peaceful as the dogs and hunters got further and further away. A deer came out of the wood and leapt the wall. The fawn ran to her and her mother licked her. They both looked at Catherine with peaceful brown eyes and then they turned and went back into the forest the way they had come.

Catherine watched them go. The doorknob creaked under her

fingers as she turned the handle to go into the cathedral.

♦ ♦ ♦

James was coming towards her.

'I've been looking all over for you. Where've you been?'

Catherine smiled, 'Back into the past. I'll tell you all about it later. It was nice this time and not scary at all.'

James smiled. 'Never a dull moment when I come out with you. Anyway, we're lucky to still have the cathedral,' said James.

'Why?'

'German planes were overhead going to bomb it flat in World War Two, but it was foggy that night so they had to go back to Germany.'

'Wow, how did you know that?'

'I just read it on a poster up there.'

She gave him a thump, 'and I thought you were so clever.'

She and James walked through the cathedral, stopping to read a page that a monk had written long ago. It was about a deer that had sought sanctuary in the cathedral when chased by hunters.

Catherine smiled,' I already knew that story,' she said.

'You and your mysteries,' James smiled back at her. 'Let's go down to the Crypt café and get some ice cream.'

Chapter 10 - The Kite Festival

Catherine felt the ten-pound note in her pocket. More and more people bumped against them hurrying excitedly as they joined the crowd going to the Kite Festival field.

The sun shone and the strong wind was ideal for kite flying. The sky was filled with kites of every colour. An octopus soared into the air dragging its tentacles behind. A sea horse bobbed on one leg. The psychedelic nylon colours of orange, blue, and yellow shone together. Every colour you could think of. The kites swooped and dived in the sky as if they were alive.

'Why've we got to get back early today?' Asked Henry.

'There's a surprise!'

The Japanese World Champion will give us an exhibition of kite flying, the loudspeaker announced. A huge kite went straight up then swooped down and to the left and right with wonderful movements. It was a Japanese man with black eyebrows and a beard that turned down at the sides. He looked strange and threatening.

'Wow! Said Henry, 'I'd like to fly my kite like that.'

They went to the Japanese tent and bought fish rolled in seaweed.

'What's this black stuff? It looks like bin liner.'

'It's seaweed,' said Catherine, sinking her teeth in. 'Tastes good.'

'Not bad,' said Henry. 'Fish and chips are better.'

They queued to get their names written in Japanese writing. The woman used a brush and ink to do it.

A man in a dark suit carrying a large brief case pushed past them nearly knocking Catherine down. 'He's in a hurry,' Catherine said rubbing her arm.

Henry bought a skeleton kite. He shook it at Catherine.

'Scary, or what?'

She laughed and shook the skeleton's hand and was surprised not to feel sick or like falling.

'I'm off to fly my kite,' said Henry.

'See you back here,' said Catherine, 'I'll go and buy one.'

There was a text message from Claire. When are you coming home? Lots happening down here. Saw Richard yesterday. He wanted to know how you were getting on and when you were coming back. He said he couldn't wait to see you. Lucky you. I told him you were having lots of adventures. See you soon.

She went into a tent to choose a kite. It was like a colourful cave stuffed full of kites or plastic bags holding kites. The inside was covered in lengths of bright material hanging from the ceiling for people to make their own kites. Every small space was covered with kite materials. You could hardly move in the tent for them. The wind shook and blew them.

Catherine noticed a furtive man at the back holding an expensive kite. It was the man who had nearly knocked her down in the Japanese tent. He glanced around and Catherine looked quickly away. She wondered why he had such a large brief case with him. Now she knew. He picked up another two kites. She suspected he was going to steal them but did not know what to do about it. She dare not tackle him herself. She looked around the tent hoping to see the owner but she was nowhere to be seen. Catherine was afraid to go for help in case the man got away.

The table was covered in kites. One was a fish with a huge pink mouth and orange body. Everything was in bright tough nylon. A woman in an orange anorak was talking to her husband about buying a kite. She could ask them for help but before she could do anything they walked out without even glancing back.

She looked up and was relieved to see James at the front of the stall. He signed 'Hello,'

She signed back, 'Bad man, stealing.'

James looked shocked then signed back. 'OK. I'll get help.'

Catherine hung around nervously pretending to look at the kites. She rubbed the orange and yellow kite material between her fingers pulling at the ropes that held them to the tent. The sun went in and it was hard to see what was going on at the back of the tent. It was like a dark cave. The wind gusted pulling at the guy ropes that held the tent as if it would rip up the tent pegs.

She would have to go further into the tent to watch the man. She inched slowly along the stall. There he was, in a dark suit carrying a large brief case. What if she was wrong and he was not stealing? He looked important and she could get into trouble if she was wrong, but she didn't think she was. She tried not to look at the man too much in case he became suspicious but she didn't want him to slip out when she wasn't looking.

She jumped when she felt a rough tongue lick her finger. It was Cindy, James's dog, drawing attention to her, just when she was trying not to be noticed. Cindy jumped up at her. 'Down Cindy, down,' she whispered. Cindy barked loudly making for the entrance to the tent. Catherine wanted to follow her to make sure she didn't get lost, but she dared not leave the tent in case the man got away.

As if suddenly making up his mind the man shoved another two kites into his briefcase and pushed his way straight towards her. Her heart was beating fast and her hands were sweating but he took no notice of her and pushed past. James and the Security Officer loomed up.

The Security Officer stepped forward, took hold of his arm and said, 'what's your hurry?' and took him away.

James patted Catherine on the back. 'Well done,' he said. 'I was worried about leaving you here with that man. He could have hurt you.'

'It's OK. You had to go for help,' said Catherine. 'I was fine.' She did feel a bit wobbly but wasn't going to say so.

The woman who owned the stall came up and shook Catherine's hand. 'I can't thank you enough,' she said. 'This is my first day with the stall and I can't afford to lose anything. I was only away for a few minutes getting change from the next tent. Please take this kite as a thank you. It's a sports kite, a Flashback. I fly one myself in the competitions. It soars like a bird.'

Catherine put her hand on it. 'It's great, thank you.' It was green, blue and purple.

Henry came rushing back, 'What's going on?' He asked.

'Don't ask,' said Catherine. 'I've been frightened nearly to death. A man was trying to steal some really expensive kites. I was afraid he would turn nasty. James and a Security man stopped him getting away. I've been given this new kite so I've still got my ten pounds.'

Henry whistled appreciatively. 'A Flashback. I've always wanted one.'

'Let's go and try it out.'

In the middle of the field they tilted the kite backwards and Catherine pulled on the lines to make them taut then she swept her arms down and backwards and the kit soared into the air like a wild thing. She kept her hands even to keep it steady until it was safely in the air then she pulled back with her right hand and the kite soared right, and then with her left hand and it flew left. She pulled on one line so that the kite looped. It responded straight away, like a live thing.

On the way home Catherine realised she had not gone back in time. Perhaps she didn't need to any more. Mrs. Tate, her history teacher, said that people who were not interested in history didn't deserve a future. Maybe she herself had learnt all she could from the past.

She and Henry ran back up the road anxious to tell Gran and Granddad about the excitement. They stopped abruptly when they turned the corner into the street. There was a car at the door. A red car. Mum's car! The sun came out brightening everything in the street.

They ran on and Mum was on the doorstep waiting for them. She hugged them both. Catherine looked anxiously into her face, but she looked great. Perhaps she was a bit thinner, but otherwise the same as always.

'This is your surprise,' said Gran smiling.

'I'm feeling great,' said Mum, 'I've come to take you home.'

'James is coming to say goodbye,' said Gran.

'I've heard a lot about him,' said Mum. 'I'll have to meet him.'

'Who told you about him?' asked Catherine.

'I can have chats with Claire as well as you,' said Mum smiling.

Catherine blushed red.

Granddad looked sad.

'Did you like the Secret Kingdom?'

'Yes, it's great but the Smoke is nice as well.'

'Smoke? What's that?'

'That's what we call London.'

'We'll come down and see what it's like. You can show us some good places to visit.'

'William I can't believe you're saying that after the things you've said about London.'

Granddad looked embarrassed. 'Everyone can change, whatever age they are.'

Catherine put her hand on Mum's short hair.

'It suits you like that.'

'It's as short as yours now, Catherine.'

'We'll be like twins,' said Catherine.

'I don't think so,' said Mum, 'Not with my wrinkles.'

There was a knock on the back door and James came in.

'Just in time to take a photo,' he said snapping Catherine and Mum together.

'James's Mum said they would all come down to London for a holiday,' Mum said. Catherine looked surprised. 'Gran gave me their number one night when I rang up to speak to you.'

The back door flew open again and a huge brown body launched into the small kitchen nearly sweeping the tea things off the table with her tail.

'Down,' shouted Granddad.

'You're like that dog,' said Gran. 'Your bark is worse than your bite.' Every one laughed at that.

'I got some good news from the hospital,' said Mum. 'I got the All Clear.' Just then the bells started up. *All clear, All Clear*, they seemed to ring out.

Mum hugged them all again.

'Soppy,' said Granddad.

Catherine remembered the All Clear when she went back to the

War and they could all come out of the dark, damp shelter.

The bells rang out again.

'What will you miss most about the North East,' Gran asked?

'Your Yorkshire puddings,' said Henry.

'We'll be back next summer holidays, of course,' said Catherine smiling around the table at them all.

The End

About the author:

Anne Colledge was born in Ruabon, North Wales, and was educated at Homerton College, Cambridge and Sunderland University. She has an honours degree in Psychology and English.

Now retired, Anne taught deaf children for thirty years. She loved working with the pre-school children: the youngest was only four months old. The children called her 'The Toy Lady' since her car was always full of toys. Anne has a high tone hearing loss herself and has two hearing aids

Anne loves reading, cycling and kayaking. She is a two-star British Canoe union canoeist, and belongs to Croquet Canoe Club. She canoes rivers, and on the sea.

Anne has five grandchildren, two in Britain, and three in America. They call her Grandma Surf, because she loves to surf.

Also by Anne College:

Northern Lights

Matthew is a deaf boy who has exciting adventures, meeting Freddie the dolphin, encountering a mine that is about to explode, and visiting the famous Farne Islands.

Northern Lights is a book for children aged eight and over.

'Exciting!' *Ann Faundez, Junior Education, Scholastic*

'Excellent!' *Deaf Education through Listening and Talking*

'A beautiful book' *Leslie Kircloff-Fawcett, President, Americ-Corp Speech and hearing.*

Published by Pipers' Ash Ltd.
www.supamasu.demon.co.uk
ISBN: 1-902-628-75-6

Printed in the United Kingdom
by Lightning Source UK Ltd.
103222UKS00001B/211